I0692286

ORIGINAL STORY BY OGDO

MENIK

THE LITTLE MAMMOTH

Translated & Illustrated by Timur Akhmedjanov
Edited by Matthew Traver

THE PRIZE FOR THE BEST CHILDREN'S BOOK IS AWARDED TO THE CONTESTANTS
OF THE LITERATURE CATEGORY FOR WORKS FOCUSED ON CHILDREN'S TOPICS
AND WRITTEN IN ANY LANGUAGE OR GENRE.

HERTFORDSHIRE PRESS

Published in United Kingdom
Hertfordshire Press Ltd © 2017
e-mail: publisher@hertfordshirepress.com
www.hertfordshirepress.com

MENIK
THE LITTLE MAMMOTH
original story by OGDO©

English

Translated & Illustrated by Timur Akhmedjanov
Edited by Matthew Traver
Design by Aleksandra Vlasova
Project manager Anna Lari

British Library Catalogue in Publication Data
A catalogue record for this book is available from the British Library
Library of Congress in Publication Data
A catalogue record for this book has been requested

ISBN 978-1-910886-62-5
PAPREBACK RRP: £ 12.50

CONTENTS

CHAPTER I
THE BEGINNING OF GLORIOUS DAYS

From this day onward, you are not allowed in my room, ever! Veronica shouted, huffing and puffing at the doorstep, just as she arrived home from school. In each hand she held a pot of flowers.

"Now why is that?" asked her grandmother in shock. "And why the flowers? Our house is already full of those."

"Gran, today in biology Mrs. Eve Kirilova told me that my grandfather is a scientist… but I, myself, have not done a single experiment. So, from now on, I'm going to study science."

"Ohh…" sighed her grandmother. "Well, what else is there left to do."

"Anyone who comes in my room, comes in with a smile" continued Veronica, "because I'm going to grow a flower full of happiness. But grandfather's room is going to be the room of anger, there I'm going to grow my second flower, and every day I'm going to shout and tell it off. And then I'll compare them, to see which one grew the most."

This conversation happened about a year ago. Neither her grandmother or grandfather could take her words seriously, but this was a huge mistake. Starting from October, for the whole year, without missing a single day, Veronica kept watch over her experiment with the flowers. But her grandfather, a scientific associate at the University of Permafrost, had also keenly kept watch over his granddaughter.

Veronica managed to write a whole report last year. She then took that report to the school meetings and conferences in Moscow. Everyone praised her there, including Mrs. Eve Kirilova. Ever since that day there has been a shift in attitude in her home. Even at the age of twelve, she was able to discover how effective growing flowers were for creating a good mood. You wouldn't believe it, but the flower of happiness had shot up to an impressive seventy centimeters in height… while the second one, in her grandfather's angry room, had somehow only managed to reach a miniscule fifteen centimeters.

Nevertheless, the trouble had only just begun. This year, Veronica and her classmate, Boris, decided to start a new experiment…

CHAPTER II
THE SECRET OF SCIENCE

It's quite important that you don't share the result of your studies too early" said Mrs. Eve Kirilova, "the more knowledge, the more interference.

But who is to say she is right? So, before starting their experiment, Veronica and Boris went into the woods, away from prying eyes, set up a fire and swore an oath over the flame. "No one except for us should know about this, no one should see, no one should hear…"

From that day on, they begun to text vigorously among each other. And the grown-ups didn't have a clue on what was going on.

"Are you WhatsApping again? Who's going to end up washing the dishes?" questioned her grandmother with a resentful tone. She had recently come to think that Veronica was becoming very lazy, for all she seemed to do was eat hastily and then run up to her room – she never helped around the house! Although, what she didn't know was that each day she was informing Boris on what tasks she had accomplished. But, what exactly were those tasks? Well, you're about to find out!

Have you heard about Yuka? Baby Mammoth Yuka? By the way, Selii, in Yakut, means mammoth. It's important you know how these ancient titans are called in the land from which they originate, this land. Thousands of people have already 'greeted' the mammoth at the local fare, including Veronica and Boris, and it was here that something popped into their heads simultaneously. They had a thought, or more accurately, an audacious idea; what if you could clone him?

"We can do this in grandfather's science lab," shouted Veronica, and then they continued in a whisper together - you wouldn't understand a word they were saying, no matter how hard you tried, trust me! As for how they got the cloning devices… I can't tell you either, it's a secret.

From that day on, they regularly went to a secluded lab located in the basement of the University of Permafrost. No other lab like this exists on the planet!

In a tightly sealed test tube the size of a bucket, something was bubbling and concealed by steam.

It was hard to see what it was, but it was clear that something was growing.

Scientists clad in wise-looking coats, hard hats and boots, crossed paths with Veronica and Boris on a daily basis in the staircase leading down into the university's lab. No one was surprised by the pair, and especially Veronica, for everyone knew her well. On the other hand, they did not know much at all about Boris.

Out of interest, do you have an idea of how clones are created? Have you ever tried to clone something yourself? I'm guessing not, and the same goes for our young and ambitious duo. At some point they will hit a dead-end and ponder on a solution. And don't forget, they can't ask anybody for help because Eve Kirilova warned them - speak with any grown-up and say goodbye to your little experiments!

They had to go to the library to find answers to their questions. You might be asking yourself, why don't they use the internet? But, the truth is not everything can be found there.

By the way, it turns out people already thought about cloning as far back as the 10th Century. Though it wasn't until now, a whole millennium later, that someone finally worked up the courage to actively begin experimenting!

CHAPTER III
HE'S NOT JUST A CLONE!

Veronica lives on the university's grounds and that's why she manages to go to the underground laboratory twice a week. Boris was less fortunate in this respect. You cannot go every day to the lab from the other end of the city, so he had to settle for one visit every Sunday. Oh, what would they do without WhatsApp?

"Boris, the test tube seems to be a little too small again ..."

"That's as it should be. Next time we will move it, but make sure to measure it."

What was in the test tube had clearly changed and condensed, absorbing all the liquid that was there. Boris, putting on his gloves, handed Veronica the test tube, and pulling on his medical mask he extracted all of the contents with tweezers and put it in a bigger one as carefully as possible.

"Damn... it has turned so stiff! Last time it was like cottage cheese, and now... now it's like meat."

"Oh, then the cells have accustomed to the conditions!"

"Be quiet! It's too early to get your hopes up! We must first observe how it grows."

"Why 'be quiet'? Science has proved that with a child, it is necessary to begin to talk to it before it's born, and the earlier, the better. So, please do not call him a devil anymore. He needs to be given a human name, so maybe he'll understand that we are addressing him."

"That's quite a good idea. Our clone is not just a clone, but a Yuka of the 21st Century, and he will not be some any old mammoth, but a clever, trained one..."

"Yes! And he must understand Yakut, because our language is also very ancient."

"It's decided. You name him, and I'll try to find out how to develop his intellect."

CHAPTER IV
THE BEGINNING OF A LEGEND

Today I have replaced the fourth test tube. The clone grew by five centimeters... the nutrient solution has almost run out, it's about time we make a new one, noted Veronica in her book.

"'Clone', 'brother'... why is there still not a name?" she muttered.

"I can't think of one! You're not just going to call him Selii, are you?!" joked Boris.

"Oy, hold on! Hold on to it tight! Boris... he just moved!"

"Oh no he didn't, your hands are just shaking"

"No, they're not! It's him! I felt it."

"Ugh, damn you... he's already fooling around!"

"Boris! There it is now! A name! We thought of a name for him! If he's such a fool, then let it be Menik!"

"You know what, it's a good name. I like it. Oh, look, I just came up with this poem right now:
Mammoth Menik, dear.
Test tube grown to be the one.
You don't look like anyone here.
Though tusks you have none."

Boris retorted. "Well right now he doesn't have any tusks, but he will grow some, and boy they will be big! And he himself will be massive, and everyone will gaze at him and be very proud. Don't worry, I'll come up with some poem as well, just wait a little bit."

A few moments passed as Veronica gazed into space, thoughtfully considering her words.
He will grow up big,
With Tusks – oh-oh-oh,
And everyone will laugh and jig
And even the boys will know"

"We do not have to write poetry right now! But I know how to make it the cleverest mammoth in the world! What's the use of a brainless mammoth? So, we will teach him. We'll tell him everything... well, not everything, but the right things."

After this conversation, Veronica and Boris having barely descended into the laboratory, repeated aloud everything that they had learned themselves. Boris even wrote a special program for the mammoth, so even in their absence he could develop and absorb valuable information.

One day though, after transferring to a new test tube, Veronica was tidying up in the laboratory whilst telling the mammoth about songs, dances, fashion and types of art, Boris suddenly exploded with rage.

"What are you trying to do? Make him a girl? He doesn't need these girly things; dances, prances, skirts... we agreed to teach him only the important and necessary things!"

"Well, how do you propose we walk around town with him? With all the shops around, if he does not know anything about fashion, he will get scared and run away..." argued Veronica.

"Why are you taking him to town anyway?!"

"You never know... in life, anything can happen. And we decided that he would live for a long time, longer than us, for at least several centuries, right? So, he must be ready for anything."

Boris felt overwhelmed with frustration, "you women are so stubborn! I don't want you to clog his brain with your rubbish! First of all, he needs to know about all types of weapons, about traps, chains, predators - there are so many dangers out there for him! He must also know to which tribe he belongs... although there are none left of his kind..."

"Do you think he needs to be afraid of everything? In life, there are not only dangers, but there are also a lot of good things. Don't scare him. And, for example, he still needs to know about art. What if he suddenly decided to become an artist? What if he chooses to perform in the circus and become a star, eh?" she thoughtfully responded.

This was their first argument in over a year.

CHAPTER V
THE AWAKENING

However, arguments are just arguments, and the experiment must carry on, especially since the last measurements showed that the mammoth significantly increased in size and looked like an actual mammoth: legs, head, hair - everything was in place. He was now in need of a test tube the size of a barrel, in order to give him room to wriggle around.

Veronica, almost buried in books, busied herself making notes. She brought them to Boris, and on the basis of her findings, he crafted up a further plan of action.

"According to my calculations, in about a month, Menik will blossom... that is, he will be born. But where will we keep him then?" Boris whipped off his gloves, put them in his pocket, pulled the mask off his face and sneezed. It was October and winter struck early this year, snow fell endlessly and the wind roared, biting at the skin. However, Boris had not been careful and ended up catching a cold.

"We'll make a small barn for him, there's a suitable place nearby" said Veronica, who had already planned ahead, smiling with joy. What a good girl she was, taking care of everything!

Later on, after their talk, poor Boris became very ill and had to stay in bed to rest, so Veronica had to do all of the work for a little while. Finally, one day she noticed an unusual activity in the test tube; Menik flinched, as if he was wounded, his sides jerking up suddenly.

"What's wrong? Perhaps Boris infected him? I told Boris, once he fell ill, to stop coming here for his own sake!"

It was late and Veronica had to go home despite the fact that she felt very nervous. Soon as the door closed behind her, the test tube staggered on the table. It seemed ridiculous for a beastly mammoth to keep growing inside a piece of fragile glass. He wanted to take a breath of fresh air, get up on his feet and warm up. Menik was suffering under the heavy pressure, when suddenly the tube cracked, splitting in half with liquid pouring over the floor – it was then he found himself lying in a large puddle on the ground.

CHAPTER VI
BIG TROUBLE

For a mammoth, even a small one, these were just doors and locks? There was only one… heavy doors that were to be knocked out with one blow!

Bang!

Menik found himself outside, under the dark night sky. He blinked, trying to make out in the glow of the street lamps exactly what was ahead of him.

What… or who could it be? Oh my, yes… it's mum! His mother! With a joyful cry he rushed to her, "I'm here, mummy!". Although he said this with a little roar, Menik was still frightened. His thick, long fur dampened by the last streams of fluid from the test tube were quickly turning into hoarfrost.

"Mother! Or are you father?" Menik hesitated. In truth, he did not know how his father was different from his mother. Veronica did not mention this before to Menik, and Boris apparently forgot to include this information in his program.

"Look, I look like you! Like for like!" he exclaimed.

Although Menik tried his hardest to pronounce the words that he had become accustomed to hearing, his best efforts resulted in a strange hollow sound, which frightened him. And his supposed mother or father, stood silent, towering over him, neither breathing nor even looking in his direction!

Menik let out a small sigh, and the steam curled over him in the air. He was completely out of breath from running around looking for his mother, but now that he had warmed up he decided to act more boldly – he went very close, poked his trunk into what he thought was her thick-coated fur and… oh! It was cold and hard. "Shouldn't my mum be warm and soft?" he thought. "So, this mustn't be her. This is a monument, or a picture, or something…" Upon realising this he was so sad that he walked away without looking back.

"Mammoth Menik, dear.
Test tube grown to be the one.
You don't look like anyone here.
Though tusks you have none."

This suddenly arose from his memory, and Menik gasped with resentment. He somehow thought that outside his glass house an interesting and cheerful life awaited him, but in reality he was alone and not needed, even by his own mother...

In the meantime, the residents of the nearby houses, frightened by the terrible, bewildering roar from the street, called the police. And very soon a flashing car appeared on the horizon, breaking the nocturnal silence with the howl of its siren. Menik sensed the danger, and with all his strength rushed to the side of the road where his so-called mother gazed coldly in the direction of the reed thickets rimming the frozen lake.

The next morning the whole institute received the news that unknown intruders had penetrated into the underground laboratory at night. They did not break the door, but demolished it completely! Equally as bad was the fact that summer was right around the corner, and if even a tiny trickle of warm air penetrated into the laboratory, all the scientific work would be wiped out. As no evidence was found, they installed a new door which was stronger than the old one, and didn't even bother to think about anything else...

Veronica and Boris had the hardest time. Menik, despite only recently being born, managed to disappear from the face of the earth!

To make things worse, that night more snow fell, covering up all his tracks. Where could they find him now? They thought hard about it, not knowing that poor Menik was buried in the reeds and stones within the snowdrift, just a few steps away from the institute. As soon as the flashing, howling car disappeared into the darkness, the mammoth turned on his back and fixed its eyes on the sky. As the sky gradually cleared of clouds, the stars began to flicker, and slowly something big, bright and round appeared. Menik didn't realise he was looking at the moon, but he was so entranced by it that he began to recall a very early memory of Veronica's words, "one must always reach out to the light, the light, the beautiful light". But how do you reach it, if it's so far away?

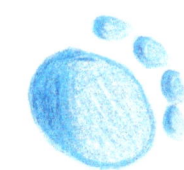
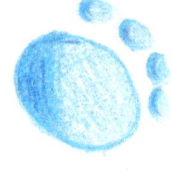

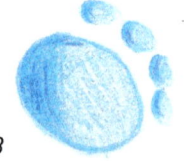

CHAPTER VII
ON THE KANKAMEE RIVER

The light streamed from the sky quietly and little Menik remembered the tale Veronica had told him some time ago. The tale was about a poor girl, who was treated very badly, and how she walked along the moonlit path into the sky.

"I would have gone too." Menik sighed, and before he could think about it anymore, this very path arose before his eyes! It really did go there, into the heights. The little mammoth watched in fascination at the way it opened right before him.

"I'll go there!" he said loudly (or rather, honked) and took his first step towards the unknown…

The invisible beast walking along the magic path felt a troublesome breeze that seemed to tease him. At first it began to blow at him slowly, then more and more intensely. The frightened Menik felt the path that he was so confidently stomping upon suddenly disappear from under his feet. An unknown force twisted and turned him around, and then he was thrown upside down, only to then be whisked away in the air like a leaf in the wind.

He flew for a long time. Barely breathing, Menik began to think what a mess he had gotten himself into. He remembered Boris had said something about the power of cars and tractors, but clearly the force that caught him was neither of those!

From time to time, impossible things can happen in nature. For example, gigantic hail might one day fall. But, never before has a hailstone the size of a baby mammoth plopped down into the Kankamee River.

A wood grouse was peacefully settling down to sleep, when suddenly… plop! A fallen 'hailstone' stirred and suddenly came to life. The wise wood grouse stepped back cautiously, and took stock of this beast with long thick fur, a large head and curious shining eyes. When the beast shook himself free of the snow, and sounded a blow across the whole forest, the grouse got so frightened that all of its feathers stood on end.

Menik did not notice the bird hiding in the snow because before him was a road - smooth, wide, and looking more solid, and reliable than the moonlit path. "It will surely be a pleasure to walk this way," thought Menik, as he started to walk on it. But very soon after walking on this iron-hard icy surface, all

four of his soles began to cramp, so he hurried off to the side and broke through the snowdrifts once more.

How long he walked for, he did not know. He was tired and hungry - he hadn't even had a sliver of food since the moment he was born! Yes, and he had wanted a drink for a long time as well... But, as soon as he entered the forest, he smelled something. Of course, he wasn't sure what it was. Full of hope, Menik went towards the smell and found himself in front of a large snowdrift. Observing it from all sides, the mammoth jumped back and forth, but the entrance was nowhere to be found. And the smell intensified incredibly, and sounds were added to it, either rumbling or grumbling. "Hmm… no, I do not know this language," Menik mused. But you can always work out some kind of deal! You just need to wake up the one who lives under this snowdrift and get to know him... moving his forehead along the snowy wall, the mammoth got lost in a strange dwelling and found himself in a dark and warm hole, which was surprisingly quite large.

Inside Menik found the source of the smell. It was covered with the same fur as his, only much shorter. It slept soundly, obviously dreaming about something because it mumbled and grumbled, and from time to time sucked on its paw. When his eyes were accustomed to the darkness, Menik saw two

more, curled up next to the first creature. They were cubs.

Who would've ever thought the mammoth would stumble upon a bear's den? But hunger is not something to be picky about, and so, pushing the beast aside, Menik pressed next to him and licked his paw. He wanted to lick another one, but then the bear roared and jumped up, as if stung, and with one powerful blow he knocked out the uninvited guest.

Angered at being awakened from her winter slumber, she rushed after the perpetrator who dared to disturb her sleep, breaking trees and branches along the way. In horror, Menik began to run, not even noticing that the magical moonlight was slipping beneath his feet, and lifting him upwards.

CHAPTER VII
THE POLE OF COLD

Miraculously, having escaped from the terrible beast, Menik got lost and felt confused for a while, but when he came back to his senses, he felt that it was hard for him to push forward. The road along which he was walking seemed difficult, and the mammoth remembered how Veronica told him about some trains that drive faster than cars along iron tracks. "I wish I could get on one of them - I could travel far in no time," thought Menik.

Before he knew it… he seemed to be on that train! He looked around, everything was whiter than white around him.

"It doesn't smell of food here…," he moaned, as the rumbling of his empty stomach drowned out all other sounds.

Rising to his feet, he noticed that at some distance the snow seemed to be riddled with something (or someone). Following the outcome of the previous bitter experience, he did not immediately run there, but from a safe distance he began to watch the place with intrigue and soon he saw some long-legged creatures with their short, sturdy feet started scraping the snow, as if they were looking for something. They kept lowering their heads to the ground, and whenever they lifted them up again, something was in their teeth. And it crackled nicely! "They're looking for food there - and they're finding it!" Menik rejoiced, and not paying attention to the road, he rushed to these long-legged creatures.

And these were, of course, the horses of the Yakut breed, who roam freely at the Pole of Cold, in Oymyakon. They live in the harshest of frosts. Their life depends on what's under this meter-thick snow. Despite their hardy nature, even these creatures shied away at the sight of the strange beast who rushed towards them across the snow-covered field, exuding an unfamiliar smell, with his long black fur waving in the wind. An alarming neigh rang through the trees, and the frightened herd sped away.

However the mammoth was not running at them. He just wanted something to eat! When he reached the hoof-stamped snow, he saw grass sticking out from underneath. Food! At last! With an appetite he bit into it; a grimy, frozen, but remarkably delicious herb that preserved the aroma of the past summer.

Menik took notice of how the snow turned into water when he held it in his cheeks. That's great! You can eat and drink at the same time, how marvelous.

"Well, you can't possibly go hungry in this place," thought the satisfied mammoth, and he decided to take a walk around the surrounding area, and at the same time, if possible, talk to these four-legged, long-tailed ones.

This time the horses were not frightened, because he approached them calmly, and did not rush at them like an angry ape. The horses were neighing, the mammoth trumpeted, and yet the main thing they understood was that they did not need to be afraid of each other. These equine inhabitants managed to explain to the massive visitor that the strongest cold would soon strike. "So, the New Year," Menik rephrased one of Veronica's stories, "a beautiful morning at all the schools, a dazzling Christmas tree, a festive dance, and everything smells of mandarins"... if only he could try these mandarins, and in general, to see everything she spoke about… Menik sighed.

The horses, of course, did not understand why he sighed, but it was clear to them that the baby of an ancient wooly beast was feeling forlorn. So, we must help him out of compassion, and also because the sky is screeching with frost and blazing snow.

Out of nowhere, in a whirl of ice, emerged snow sledges. At the far end of the sleigh train sat a blue cloaked and bearded man. It was Chys Khan, the Lord of the Cold:

"Have you seen Kharchaa here?" he asked. "I need to find the snow maiden before the New Year."

On his head he wore a cap with fur edges and gleaming horns, and his neat fluffy coat was adorned with radiant snowflakes. Leaning on his snowflake-topped staff, he leaned toward Menik.

"Who are you? Why don't I know you?"

"I'm a mammoth. We lived on this earth once… a long, long time ago. Menik is what they called me, before I got lost…"

After saying this, the poor man almost cried. "That's it… I've seen your herds in those unforgettable times. The fiercest frosts and blizzards were almost nothing to your kind. You were the only mighty giants to live during the Ice Age. But I haven't seen your kind for thousands of years. They must have moved to the north, and if so, Cholbon Kuo should have seen your kind. Do not lose hope, believe in the future. Times are changing; magic is present and any dream can come true. No wonder they say Happy New year, because it's full of happiness!" With those words Chys Khan jumped into his sleigh and soared away in o the snowy sky.

CHAPTER IX
ON LAKE LABYNKYR

After the meeting with Chys Khan, Menik began to feel joyous, and so began to cheerfully sing (well, more like toot through his trunk):

Mammoth Menik dear.
Test tube grown to be the one,
You don't look like anyone here,
Though tusks you have none.
He will grow up big,
With tusks – oh-oh-oh,
And everyone will laugh and jig.
And even the boys will know

He was so absorbed in his song that it took quite some time for him to notice a pool of water in the middle of the snow. Menik was very surprised by it, and it looked appetising, so he dipped the tip of his trunk in. This amazing water gave him strength, and he cheerfully walked until it was completely dark, reaching the shores of a very strange lake. It was covered with snow, on which there were no tracks - neither human, nor animal. Therefore, not a single living soul came here. And it was dead silent.

Where was he now? He ruffled around through the snow, ate, laid down to rest and thought about what to do next. Darkness descended on to the ominous lake, and from the depths of the night came a terrible roar, or was it a howling? Menik didn't even know what to call it. He jumped up and with a pounding heart, peered into the inky dark that now surrounded him from every side. He could not see a single thing, until…

"Grrr! Hrrr! Arrr! Rrrr! Hiss! Baaarrkkk!"

Menik rushed about in panic, honking for help.

"Mother! Veronic-a-a-a! Boris-s-s!"

Suddenly, a thundering and rattling bellowed beneath him, and a layer of ice started to rise. Something emerged, huge and serpentine in its appearance. Streams of icy water poured off of it, splashing dirt and mud over the white snow.

It was the Labynkyr Devil!

Menik nearly fainted upon seeing this frightful creature. But, just in time, the moonlit track saved him again leading him away from this infamous aquatic ruler.

CHAPTER X
ON THE RIVER YANA

This time the moon's trail behaved calmly. Maybe it was because the frost was cracking, and there was no wind. The little mammoth, even though he managed to catch some rest along the way, still hadn't recovered from his recent beastly scare.

"Menik, in whatever mess you get, keep hold of your tail!" he remembered Boris' wise words.

"Do not give up, and you'll make it out safe and sound."

He struggled with all his might not to give up and wished for Boris and Veronica. And he still needed to find his own kind! Chys Khan said that they must have gone north. Only, how could he get there?

Menik was dejected. He dug himself in a snow shelter, and nested there so that no living soul would disturb him.

He had a dream that everything around him was blooming, green, and the aromas were making his head spin. Suddenly a beautiful butterfly flew up to him, fluttering its wings and singing.

"Our little mammoth is very tired
And hasn't slept for a while
He's inspired to search for his kind
And he will gain strength to run a mile"

Menik snorted and wriggled in his slumber. But in the background he could hear a faint voice.

"Little Mammoth, get up! Get up quickly!"

He immediately leapt up out of his hiding place onto the snow, and before him stood Kharchaa, who was surrounded by dancing snowflakes. She smile at him.

"Oh, little mammoth…"

"My name is Menik."

"Oh my little mammoth. I congratulate you this New Year! Come with me, I will show you a wonderful land!"

The mammoth did not refuse. Who does not want to see a place where miracles happen?

They climbed a high mountain, to the very top.

"This is Kisilyakh. A sacred place of power. These rocks have stood here for millions of years. Your relatives once lived here, and at the time there were so many all across Yakutia. And then, you suddenly disappeared from the face of the earth... until now! It turns out the mammoth are still well and truly alive, more alive than anyone could've imagined!"

Her eyes sparkled, and her voice became serious and strong.

"Here, surrounded by stone giants, I give you their power! Live for all of your great family, live for the glory of your native land!"

Her last words dwindled away in a whirlwind as she shrunk to the size of a snowflake and blew away into the sparkling sky.

Menik walked around the stony giants frozen in time, considering the meaning of her words, peering at every single figure, and marveling at how close the sky was from here. It was beginning to get dark, which meant that soon his rescuer will appear - the moonlit path. Maybe this time it will take him to his family? Kharchaa says that they disappeared without a trace.

And Chys Khan said that they should be sought in the far north. Who should he believe? It was hard to say, but he thought it would be worth checking north. What if one of his relatives was really there?

CHAPTER XI
THE LAPTEV SEA

Never before had the mammoth managed to reach the magical path to the moon. Halfway through he had always been blown off of it and thrown somewhere else. But now, having escaped from certain death, Menik was determined to reach the end, "if the wind tries again, I must at all costs stay on the path and walk towards its beautiful light! When I get to it, I'll ask it the most important question of all..."

As he ascended higher and higher in to the sky, the stars trembled in fear as they had never seen anything like him in their lifetime. Their trembling gave rise to countless wonderful melodies that merged into one, to create a sound so alluring that there were no words to describe it.

"It's a miracle!" Menik admired, "it's great up here!" But before he could say anymore, the magical music whipped up a ferocious wind and all of a sudden, Menik found himself on a ship bobbing on a gloomy sea. The waves swelled all around him, as if trying to drown him, but he echoed out across the water with his stubborn whistles, hoping someone would hear him.

When the ship landed on the shore, it was clear that no one was there to meet our little mammoth, so Menik again trundled forward as best he could. His sad thoughts quickly disappeared as soon as he saw some snow-covered islands, rising out from the middle of the sea. He smiled.

At first glance, he already knew from somewhere that it was the homeland of his ancestors. He was so happy! All he wanted to do now was plunge into the cold water and wash away his fears from the last few days, but he restrained himself for he was still on a mission to find his own kind.

It was a wise decision because something was lurking under the icy waters, and suddenly emerged before the amazed mammoth... a bear! It was exactly like the one he encountered in the Kankamee River den, except this one was completely white. But, the same evil was in her eyes. Instantly she exposed her fangs, growled, lowered her head and lifted her back legs. Behind her were two cubs, also curiously white in their appearance. Menik had no time think, his previous meeting with the bear was already enough excitement for him, so he bolted away in the opposite direction!

CHAPTER XII
OLENYOK

In the distance Menik could see mountains, but to get to them, it was clear he had to walk a great distance. All around him was snow, and not a single tree to be seen. Menik walked until he met a huge crowd of animals with surprising horns. He had never seen anything like it before. They seemed unafraid of him, standing stoically, licking white stones on the ground, and it was clear from their happy appearance that they really enjoyed this occupation. What he didn't know was that this was a herd of reindeer, who had only recently escaped a pack of wolves, and were now blissfully eating away at salt.

"Wow, there's a lot of them, but I'm all alone… will I ever find my own kind?" Menik thought.

The poor mammoth could not stand it and cried. The reindeer herders listened to his woeful roar and, getting ready to fight, they ran to see what danger threatened their flock. As the men arrived, they were astounded by what they saw. Before them stood a small and exhausted beast, roaring unhappily. The men surrounding Menik were terrified and unable to move a muscle.

"I don't believe it! No way, a mammoth has come to us!" one of the men shouted in astonishment.

"It seems that it has lost its mother," said another.

"Where did he come from? The mammoths died out a long time ago!" They began to argue about the living miracle of nature before them.

He felt uncomfortable watching them squabble, so plucking up the courage he decided to introduce himself, "my name is Menik. I've never met my mother before. Do you understand me?"

All the men could hear were small sighs and squeaks from the mammoth. But the reindeer herd understood, in their own special way, what he was trying to say.

"Poor thing, it's so hungry, it might die. Let's look after him and feed him" remarked one of the men before walking off to his chum to find some salt to nourish him.

Menik, who had become terribly lonely through all his wandering, followed the man. As he entered his fur covered home, he pulled back one of the skins which formed the door, revealing a television inside. Menik saw a glimpse of something on the screen, it

was the mammoth monument! A voiceover was broadcasting that scientists studying mammoths had come from all over the world, to an international scientific meeting in Yakutsk. That world now seemed so far away, where everything around him there was trying to eat him! So, he must not leave these kind people here. They will feed him and protect him.

CHAPTER XIII
IN YAKUTIA ONCE MORE

The next morning, the silence of the camp was broken by the roar of a helicopter. A rotor, lifting clouds of snow and dust into the air, landed near to the chum.

Somehow word had gotten out about Menik's arrival and, unsurprisingly, the news aroused scientists around the whole world, who were now here to meet him. A group of men lured him into a cage with a piece of salt, and after entering, he lay down quietly, ready for the long flight ahead.

Veronica and Boris also watched the news on the television and were dumbfounded! Menik? How did he manage to get all the way up to Olenka? That is some endurance and luck!

Meanwhile, the mammoth was taken from the airport straight to the university. There was a special room prepared just for him, where next to a glass window lay poor Yuka.

As he arrived people began to gawk at him. Menik could feel his eyes darken with fury, and through their maddening gasps, he could hear a sharp and abrupt command, "put him to sleep, immediately, we don't want him escaping!"

A thought flashed through his head, and tears began to roll from his eyes and onto his trunk.

"This is the end of me. It's all over. Nobody will protect me."

But no! He couldn't give up, just like that - he will smash this damned place apart, even if it kills him!

"Menik! Oh, Menik!" shouted a kind voice from the crowd. It was Veronica squeezing towards him, with Boris following behind her.

"Menik, Menik, stop!"

People parted to let them through. But, Menik did not calm down. Anger was still raging inside of him. Boris, now ahead of Veronica, ran up to the little mammoth, his tear-stained face tucked between the bars of his cage. He firmly grasped the iron with one hand, and reached in with his other hand, stretching out as far as he could to pet him.

"Menik, don't worry, it's me, Boris!"

"What is a child doing in here? Get him out

immediately!" bellowed a voice in the crowd.

Boris clasped his hand tightly on to Menik's coat, and through his tears he said:

> *"Mammoth Menik, dear.*
> *Test tube grown to be the one,*
> *You don't look like anyone here,*
> *Though tusks you have none."*

"Menik! Baby, do you remember me?" Veronica found herself next to him and, with a thin trembling voice, she spoke.

> *"He will grow up big,*
> *With tusks — oh-oh-oh,*
> *And everyone will laugh and jig*
> *And even the boys will know"*

As if awakened from a long sleep, Menik looked at them with both of his beady eyes. Here they are, Veronica and Boris, who nursed him as he was growing in a test tube, fed him and taught him everything they could! Lifting his trunk, he hooted through his tears, "where have you gone? Why did you leave me alone?"

"We did not abandon you. You ran away, silly! But, now we will never part again! It's incredible that you reached Olenka" replied Veronica, as she squeezed her narrow body through the bars of the cage.

Veronica turned to address the growing audience around them. "It's a clone of Yuka. This is his brother, Menik, now the only living mammoth in the world. We took him to the University of Permafrost's laboratory. He was born just three months ago, and unlike his ancestors, he is able to understand Yakut, which we taught him."

"So things like that can really happen!" exclaimed one of the onlookers.

And then the crowd went silent.

CHAPTER XIV
MENIK THE MIRACLE

Over the next three years, Menik was placed in the Orto Doydu, the northernmost zoo in the world, where he was carefully studied and looked after. It was clear to everyone, including Veronica and Boris, that Menik was a miracle and gift to the world! Every day they visited him, watching him as he grew up under the open sky, marveling at the thought of him living a thousand years!

MARIA SHEVEL AWARD - 2016

THE MARIA SHEVEL PRIZE was established for the first time this year. The prize is awarded to contestants in the Literature Category for works focused on children's topic and written in any language or genre.

    Maria Shevel is a Ukrainian architect (b. May 1st 1943). After graduation she departed for Central Asia to participate in the construction of the Toktogul hydroelectric power plant in Kyrgyzstan. Afterwards, in 1965, she began working under the direction of Sharf Rashidov's personal administration team in the development of the Hungry Steppe and the architectural layout of Dzhizak city in Uzbeksitan. She received numerous state awards for her work, such as the Hero of Social Labour, Retired Worker and the Motherhood medal.

ABOUT AUTHOR

This year the **Maria Shevel Prize was awarded to Yakutian writer, Evdokiya Irintseeva (Ogdo)**, for her fairy tale titled, Baby Mammoth Menik. The prize was awarded to Evdokiya by the Art Director of Hertfordshire Press, Aleksandra Vlasova. Evdokiya has dedicated her life to working with children and encouraging their creativity and works in the editor's office for Yakutia's children's newspaper, Keskil, which is distributed across the republic.

ABOUT TRANSLATOR & ILLUSTRATOR

Timur Akhmedjanov, an English teenager of Uzbek origin, currently lives with his parents in Aldbury village, Hertfordshire, United Kingdom. Growing up in a creative and well-travelled family has inspired him to become a member of the Eurasian Creative Guild, as well as a volunteer for the Open Eurasia Literature Festival and Book Forum. He has a passion for drawing, music, making films, and in the future he wants to become a cinematographer. The biggest influence on his creative life is owed to his grandmother, who was a famous town planner in Uzbekistan, along with his parents who are publishing professionals and leading figures in Europe's Eurasian community.

www.ingramcontent.com/pod-product-compliance
Lightning Source LLC
Chambersburg PA
CBHW041720240626
47171CB00002B/11